Your hand

This book needs

YOU!

What if some tiny SLUGS fell into a pool of **toxic** goo and became Giant Slugs?

What if some SPIES were sent into the JUNGLE to spy on them?

Would the Giant Slugs TAKE OVER THE WORLD?

Or would the spies vanquish them with their secret weapon?

You'll have to finish the illustrations and find out. . . .

Prepare to LAUGH while you doodle and SNICKER while you read.

Slime Sucker

INTRODUCING the Spies!

★ Gadget Gavin ★

★ Secret Steve ★

★ Agent X ★

★ Dangerous Dave ★

★ Cryptic Carl ★

MEGA MASH-UP

Spies vs. Giant Slugs in the Jungle

Nikalas Catlow
Tim Wesson

Draw your own adventure!

nosy crow™

An imprint of Candlewick Press

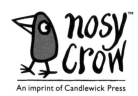

An imprint of Candlewick Press

Copyright © 2012 by Nikalas Catlow and Tim Wesson

First U.S. edition 2012

Library of Congress Cataloging-in-Publication Data is available.

Library of Congress Catalog Card Number 2012938735

ISBN 978-0-7636-5902-8

12 13 14 15 16 17 BVG 10 9 8 7 6 5 4 3 2 1

Printed in Berryville, VA, U.S.A.

This book was typeset in Agenda.
The illustrations were created digitally.

Nosy Crow
an imprint of
Candlewick Press
99 Dover Street
Somerville, Massachusetts 02144

www.nosycrow.com
www.candlewick.com

INTRODUCING the Giant Slugs!

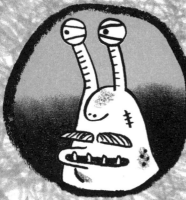

Sticky Colin

Big Suzy

Slimeball

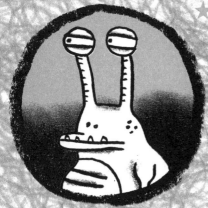

Gloop

Oozy Bob

You'll need these....

DRAWING tools

These are the **3** tools that Nikalas and Tim used to create the artwork in this book.

felt-tip pen or marker

pencil

crayon

PEN

crayon

Using different tools helps create great drawings.

texture page

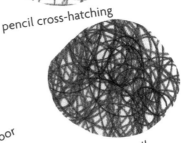

pen zigzags

crayon rubbing from linoleum floor

pencil cross-hatching

pencil rubbing from wooden door

crayon rubbing from wood floor

scribbly pencil

There are lots of ways you can add texture to your artwork. Here are a few examples.

crayon rubbing from wall

pencil dashes

pen circles

DRAWING TIP!
Turn to the back of the book for ideas on stuff you might want to draw in this adventure.

Get Ready for a Really Sketchy adventure!

Pencils at the Ready . . .

On Your Marks . . .

Let's Draw!

Chapter 1

A Toxic Goo Brew

Add woody texture to the trees.

Add JUNK to this heap.

An OIL COMPANY has been drilling in the jungle and left it in a huge mess.
Two workers are supposed to be cleaning up.
But the jungle is creepy, and they are getting SPOOKED.

Draw a ferocious bear!

Suddenly, a twig SNAPS, and out of the undergrowth comes a **HUGE BEAR**! The scaredy-cat workers FLEE IN PANIC, leaving an overturned barrel dripping **toxic goo** into a strange-looking pool.

Add more blobby mutations to the toxic goo.

Draw a slug doing the backstroke.

Some small slugs slither curiously toward the foul-smelling pool. But OOPS, they slip-slide in! The slime **bubbles** furiously . . .

… and the tiny creatures turn into GIANT SLUGS!
They ooze TOXIC SLIME, and they are **EVIL**.

GROWING

Bigger

AND EVIL

Draw your own evil GIANT SLUG!

One Giant Slug declares
himself leader.
"I am **Slimeball**!" he roars, crazed with
ambition. "Who wants to join me and
TAKE OVER THE WORLD?"

Design a
poster for
Slimeball's
evil gang!

"World domination, here we come!" cries Slimeball, cackling. "And **NO ONE** can stop us!"

Draw Slimeball as King of the World!

Chapter 2

Operation Slime Time

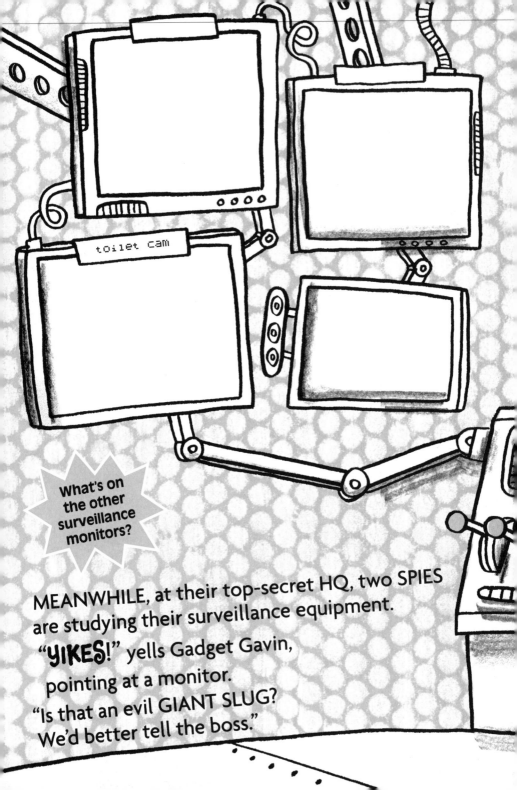

toilet cam

What's on the other surveillance monitors?

MEANWHILE, at their top-secret HQ, two SPIES are studying their surveillance equipment.

"**YIKES!**" yells Gadget Gavin, pointing at a monitor.

"Is that an evil GIANT SLUG? We'd better tell the boss."

Agent X assembles a crack team to investigate the jungle "These boys have seen more jungle action than I've had hot dinners!" he says. "Prepare for Operation Slime Time!"

PROFILE

NAME: AGENT X
EXPERTISE:

HOBBIES:

COMBAT STYLE:

NAME: DANGEROUS DAVE

EXPERTISE: SKYDIVING WITHOUT A PARACHUTE BEHIND ENEMY LINES

HOBBIES: BASE JUMPING IN A WING SUIT, KUNG FU WITH A BLINDFOLD, MOTOR RACING IN A BURNING CAR, CROCHET, AND POTTERY

COMBAT STYLE: KAMIKAZE

NAME: CRYPTIC CARL
EXPERTISE:

HOBBIES:

COMBAT STYLE:

NAME: SECRET STEVE
EXPERTISE:

HOBBIES:

COMBAT STYLE:

NAME: GADGET GAVIN
EXPERTISE:

HOBBIES:

COMBAT STYLE:

Fill in the profile sheets.

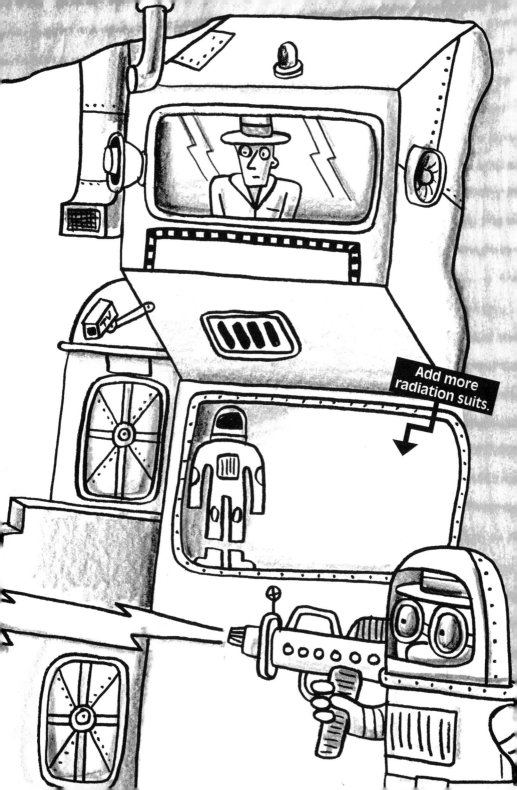

The SPIES learn about their **MISSION**.
"**GIANT SLUGS**, men," explains Agent X.
"Here's the intel."

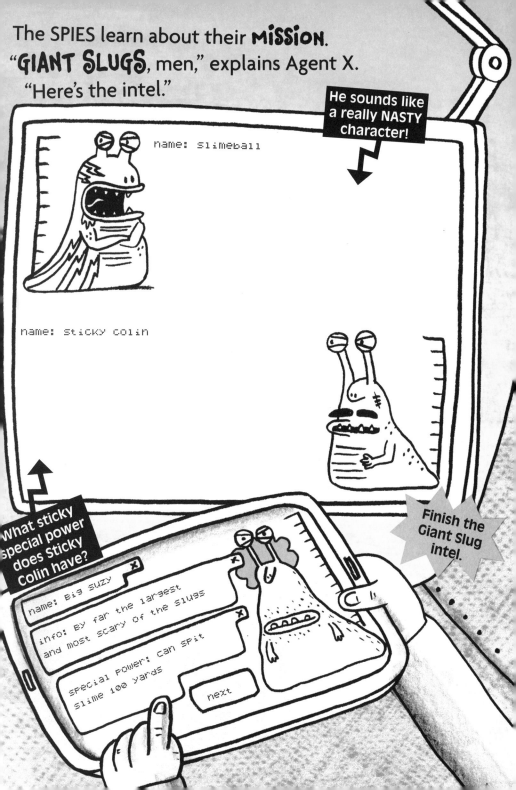

He sounds like a really NASTY character!

name: slimeball

name: sticky colin

what sticky special power does Sticky Colin have?

Finish the Giant Slug intel.

name: Big Suzy

info: By far the largest and most scary of the slugs

special power: can spit slime 100 yards

next

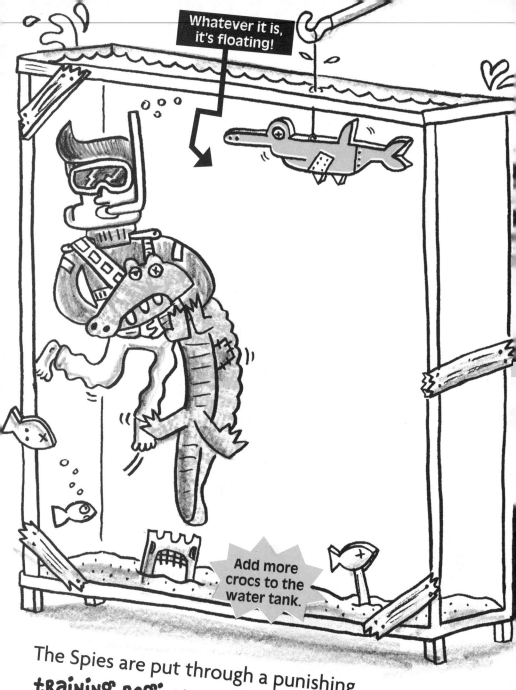

The Spies are put through a punishing **training regimen** in a controlled "jungle environment." "OK, men, pack your bags," says Agent X. "We fly to the jungle tonight."

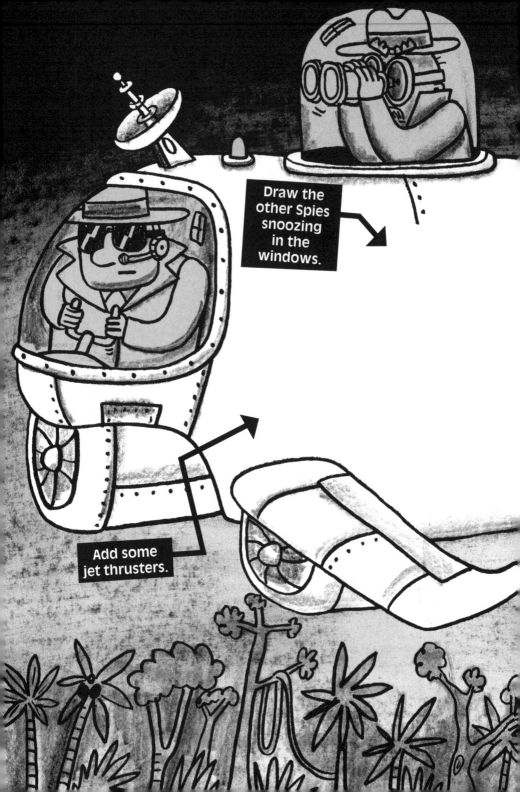

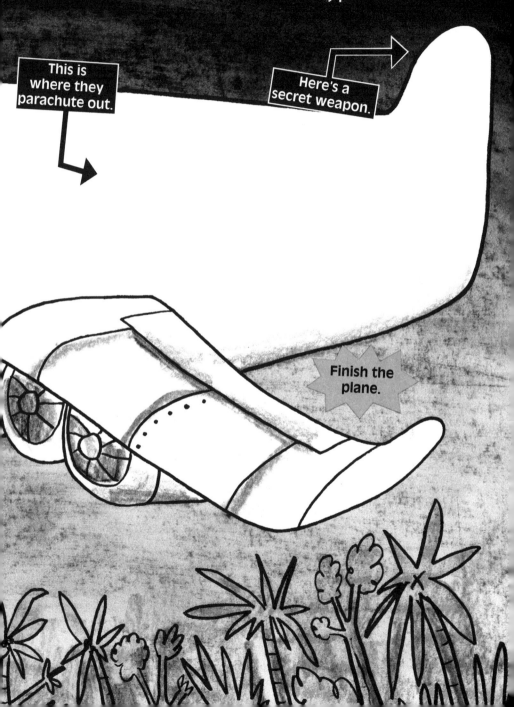

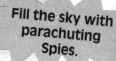

check out that cloud surfing!

The SPIES land **BEHIND ENEMY LINES**.
It's time for a rumble in the jungle. . . .

Chapter 3

Lights! Camera! Action!

The SPIES build their base camp **iN tHe tReetops**.
"I'm the King of the Swingers, yeah!"
hollers Dangerous Dave.
Agent X frowns. "Stop monkeying around!"

Here's a helicopter on a landing pad.

Finish the Spies' treetop base camp.

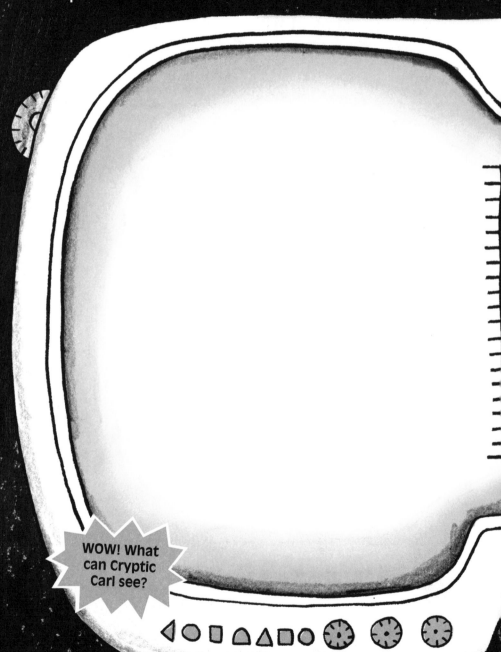

WOW! What can Cryptic Carl see?

"CRIPES!" exclaims Cryptic Carl, peering through his night-vision goggles. "What on EARTH is that?"

What is Oozy Bob thinking about?

Give Oozy Bob some oozy texture.

Suddenly a film crew bursts through the trees. "Get me **SLIME MONSTERS** or else!" screams the director. He sees the Giant Slugs. "Now, this is more like it! Great costumes, people!"

Draw another actor in a slime-monster costume.

Give the Giant Slugs some texture or shading.

The Giant Slugs go into makeup, and the director talks them through scene one. "Attack everyone, and take over the world!" he says.
"It'll be like a practice run," Slimeball says with a slimy chuckle.

What strange costume is Sticky Colin wearing?

"ACTION!" shouts the director. The Giant Slugs go berserk! **CRUNCH! SLURP! MUNCH!** They're EATING the film crew!

Yuck! The camera has been covered in toxic snot!

ROAR!

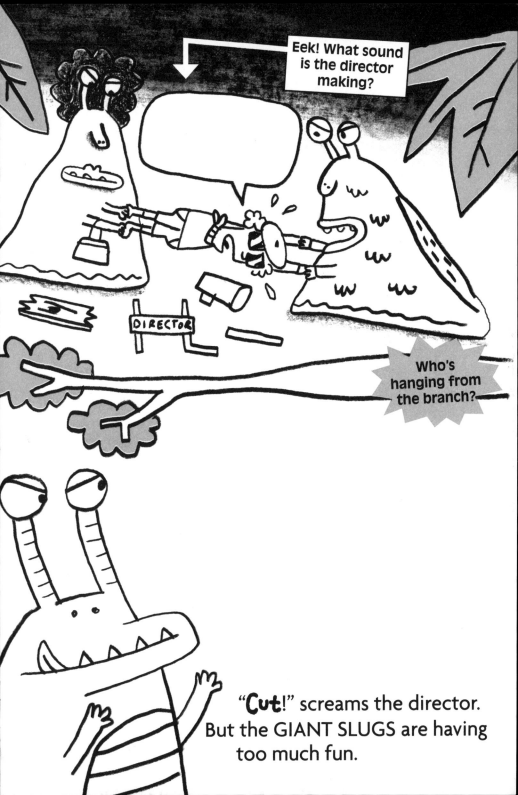

The SPIES watch the rampage in horror.
As the Giant Slugs slither off into the forest,
Oozy Bob dawdles behind.
"Fire up the Immobilizer 1000!" orders Agent X.
"We'll bring that STRAGGLER in for questioning!"

NET

PROPS

Does Oozy Bob think there's food in there?

WHOOSH! Down comes the net, and Oozy Bob is trapped!

Draw Oozy Bob wriggling in the net.

Chapter 4
There's Something Odd About Oozy Bob

"H-E-A-V-E!
H-E-A-V-E!"

"Rush this GIANT SLUG up to base for questioning!" says Cryptic Carl. "Let's hope Nellie can take the strain."

Finish Nellie.

Add texture to the elephant.

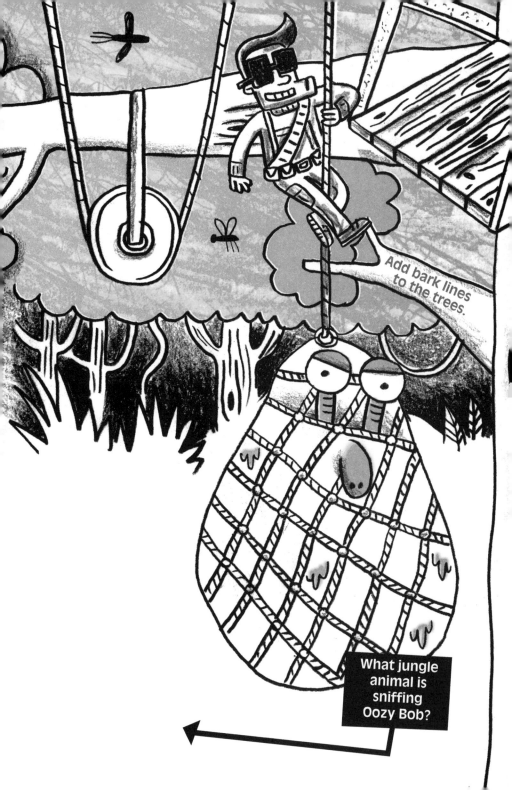

The Spies strap Oozy Bob to their
Fact Extractor.
"What's your EVIL PLAN, Giant Slug?" demands Agent X.

"**Schlerrrp!**" replies Oozy Bob.

"That's a terrible plan," points out Gadget Gavin.

Give Agent X a serious expression.

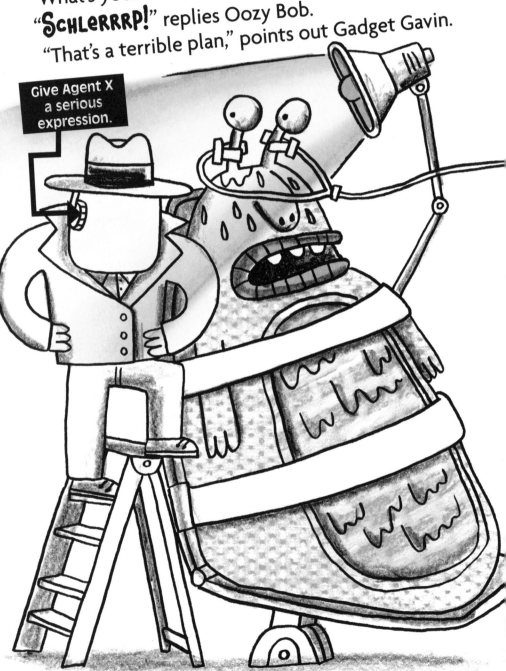

Finish the SPIES' Fact Extractor.

Cryptic Carl starts the interrogation, bombarding Oozy Bob with questions. "Why do you smell so bad?" he quizzes. "Do you eat your own boogers?" But Oozy Bob won't talk.

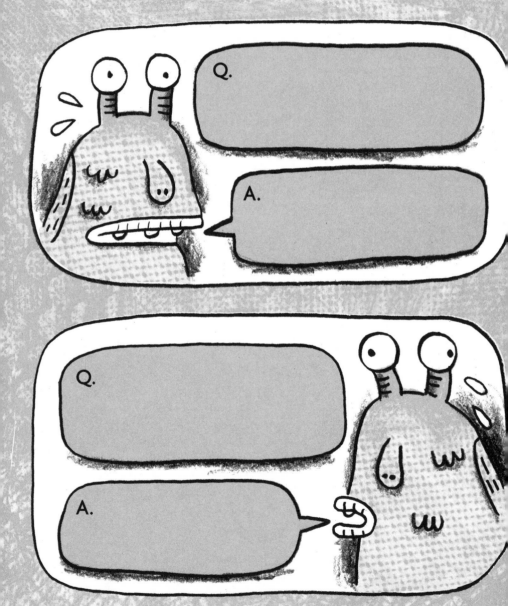

"Oh, this is useless!" yells Agent X.
"Bring in the Slug Decoy machine! We'll INFILTRATE
their slimy gang IN DISGUISE."

"Can I drive it?" asks Dangerous Dave excitedly.

"No! **You're WAY too Dangerous**,"
replies Agent X. "You get the back end!"

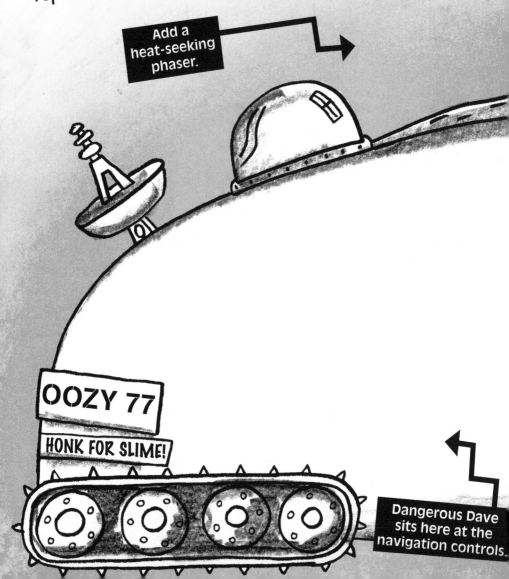

Add a
heat-seeking
phaser.

OOZY 77

HONK FOR SLIME!

Dangerous Dave
sits here at the
navigation controls.

At Camp Slug, the evil gang is studying the PLAN OF ACTION when the Slug Decoy machine rumbles in.

Add some doodles to illustrate the plan.

Plan to Invade THE CITY and Take over the World

1. Rampage into the city.

2. Get a haircut and then eat the hairdresser.

3. Slime a busload of people.

Add texture and shading to the Giant Slugs.

"Oozy Bob!" says Sticky Colin. "Where you been, man?" Then he does a double take. "You're not Oozy Bob! **Attack, attack!**"

4. Gobble up the president.

5. Terrorize lots more people.

6. Declare the world ours!

What does the Spies' radio look like?

"**MAYDAY, MAYDAY!**" Agent X radios back to the other Spies. "We've been **RUMBLED!** We'll have to make a run for it!"

Chapter 5

Slugs rule the World

The SPIES make a run for it, but the
Slug Decoy machine slows them down
and the GIANT SLUGS are right behind.
"Destroy them!" spits Slimeball.

Finish the rope-bridge maze!

Fill the pit with HUNGRY crocodiles!

The Secret Agents back at the base hear lots of snapping and screaming. **"That doesn't sound good,"** says Gadget Gavin. "Thank goodness I've been working on Plan B."

Meanwhile, the Giant Slugs are back at Camp Slug and are packing for their trip to THE CITY.
"What should I wear to take over the world?" ponders Big Suzy.
"I'm gonna eat a **Lot of HUMaNS**," Slimeball declares.

Finish this map of THE CITY.

MAP

Complete the cityscape.

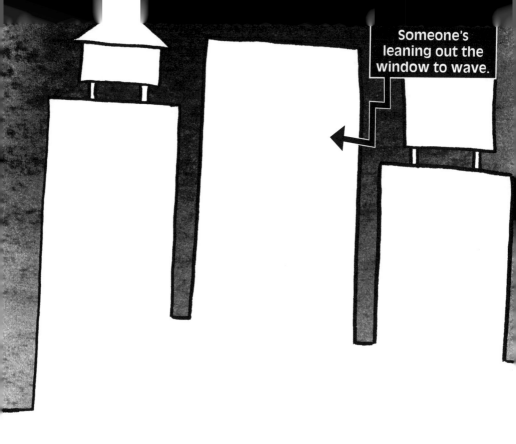

The GIANT SLUGS soon reach the bright lights of THE CITY. Big Suzy starts **DROOLING** at the thought of getting a trendy new haircut and sliming all those humans!

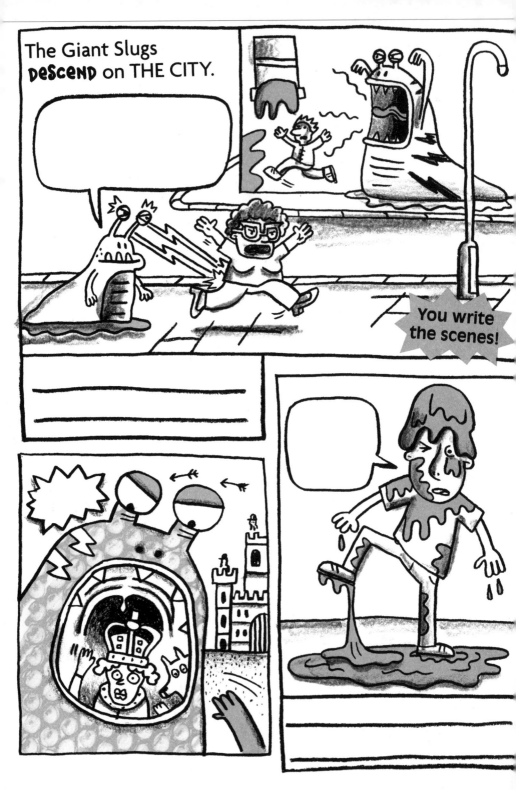

Chapter 6

Exploding Slugs!

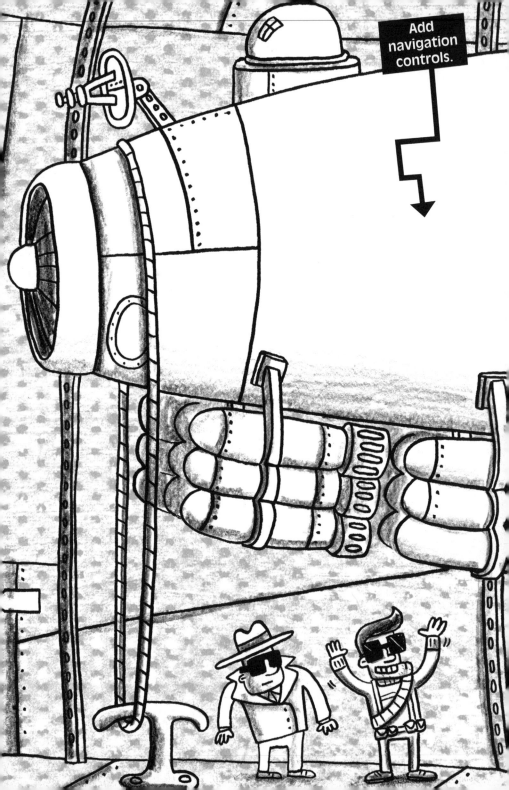

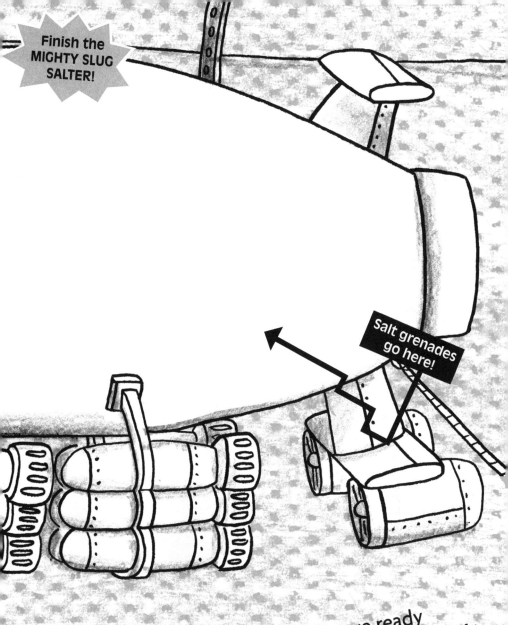

Finish the MIGHTY SLUG SALTER!

Salt grenades go here!

Meanwhile, back in the jungle, the Spies are ready for action. "**The Mighty Slug Salter is complete!**" Gadget Gavin announces. "Let the SALT ASSAULT begin!"

The **ENORMOUS ZEPPELIN** flies silently through the sky.
"The enemy has been sighted," reports Agent X.
"OK, boys, GET READY TO SLUG this one out!"

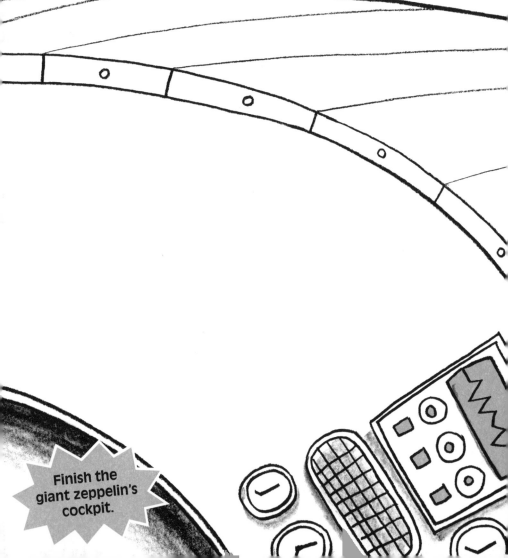

Finish the giant zeppelin's cockpit.

POP! SPLAT! The Giant Slugs **EXPLODE!** All the slimy monsters leave behind are little puddles of ooze.

What does Slimeball look like when he explodes?

POP!

SQUELCH

Slime Sucker

Who else is in the cheering crowd?

"HURRAH!"
Slugmania is no more. The Spies have saved the world from Giant Slugs!

HOW I INFILTRATED THE SLUG CAMP
by Dangerous Da
Draw the Slug Decoy machine.
A STICK
END
Draw the MIGHTY SLUG SALTER.

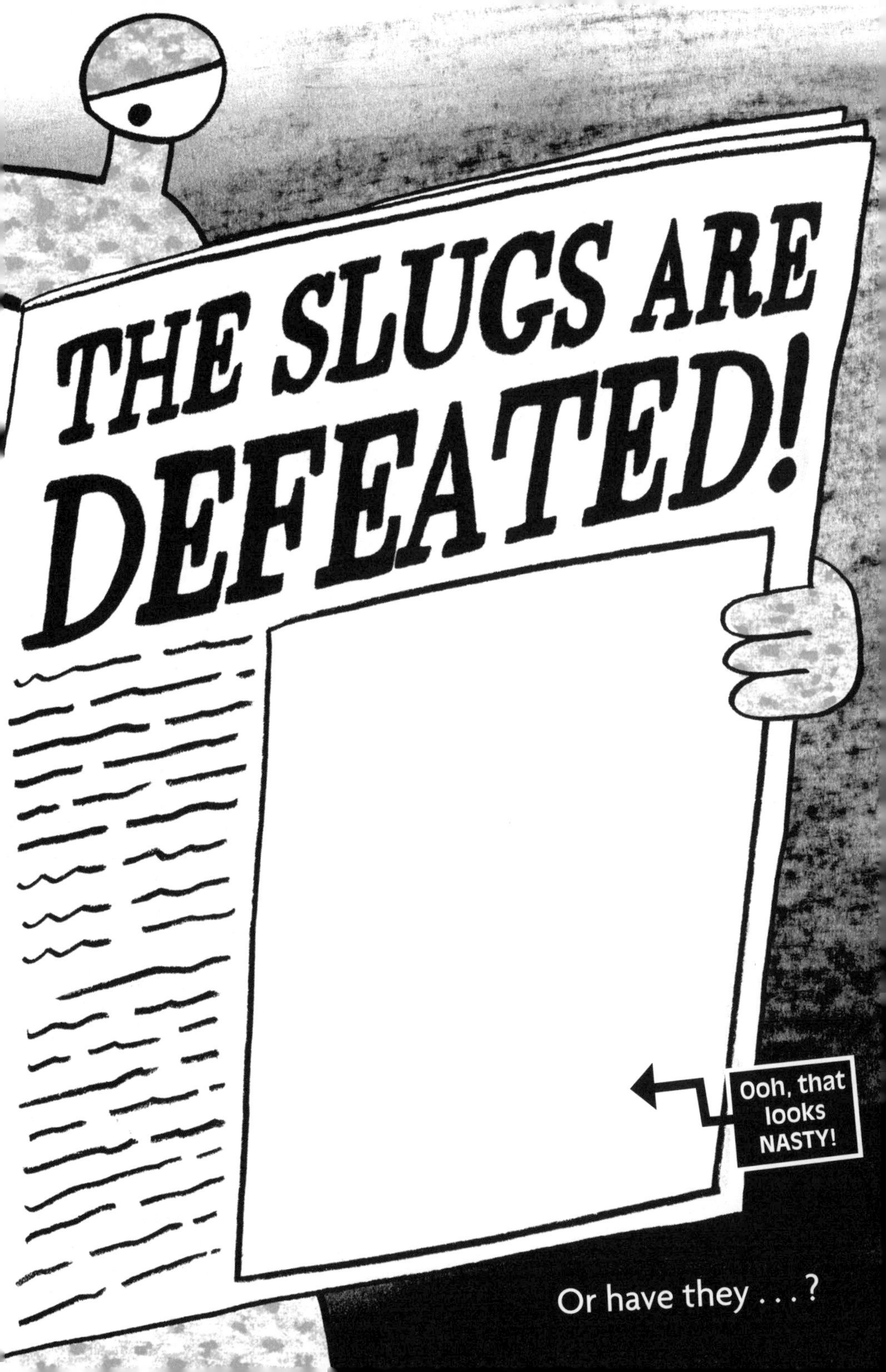
THE SLUGS ARE DEFEATED!
Ooh, that looks NASTY!
Or have they . . . ?

Picture Glossary

If you get stuck or need ideas, then use these pages for reference.

Bridge

Spies' Treehouse Parts

Communications Tower

Lookout Post

Radio Mast

If you like, you can copy the pictures. OR you can draw your own versions.

Parachuting Spies

Bits of Junk

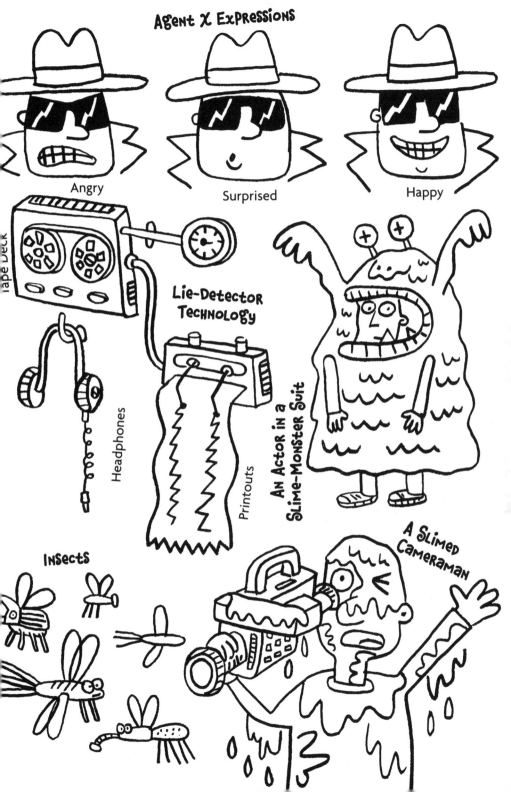

MORE Picture Glossary

Here are some more ideas.

Jet Thruster

Spy-Plane Gadgets

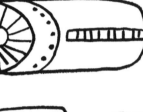

Dials and Meters

Artillery

Shrink Ray

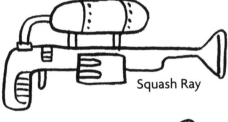

Squash Ray

Stretch Ray

If you like, you can copy the pictures. OR you can draw your own versions.

Visit our **awesome** website and get involved!

Website